PAROL

What Makes Us Filipino

Cruz. Manalo

Cruz. Manalo

DEDICATION

To our families, friends, and loved ones across the globe

Cruz. Manalo

DEDICATION

To our families, friends, and loved ones across the globe

Cruz. Manalo

THIS BOOK BELONGS TO:

_____

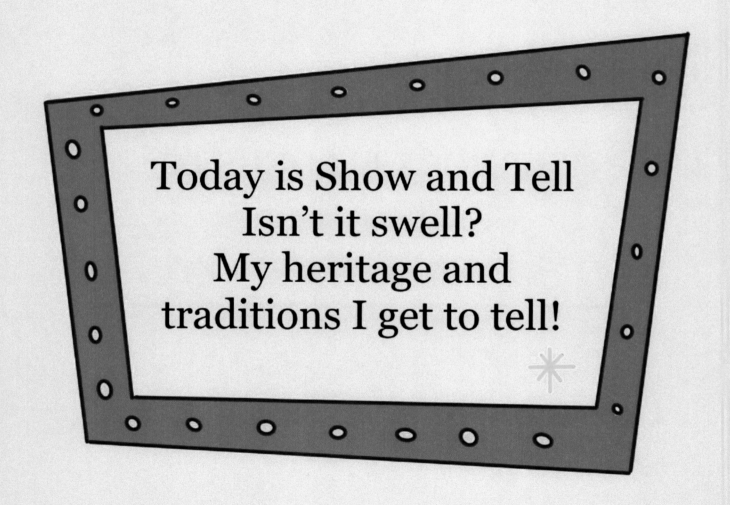

A scruffy dog
with the shiniest
mane

An orange truck

And a toy airplane

But mine is different, it looks strange
Something my whole family loves, for a change.

"Who's going first?", asked the teacher
"Me! Me!" I waved my *Parol* so eager!

My friends look at me and they all ask

"What is this star Inggo has?"

In front of everyone, here I stand
Holding this star made of
colorful paper and rattan.

*Bright light, shiny star,
that's how I know Christmas
is not that far!*

"So, why the star? What's it called?"

"Parol", I said, "You'll see it when the wind gets cold!"

Bright light, shiny star, that's how I know

Christmas is not that far!

We are always spreading goodness and joy

And for us that is very *Pinoy!*

It's a Filipino tradition to start the holidays early!

"Filipinos start the holidays early?", asked Cassie

I smiled so proudly, *"Why yes we do, and it's all so fancy!"*

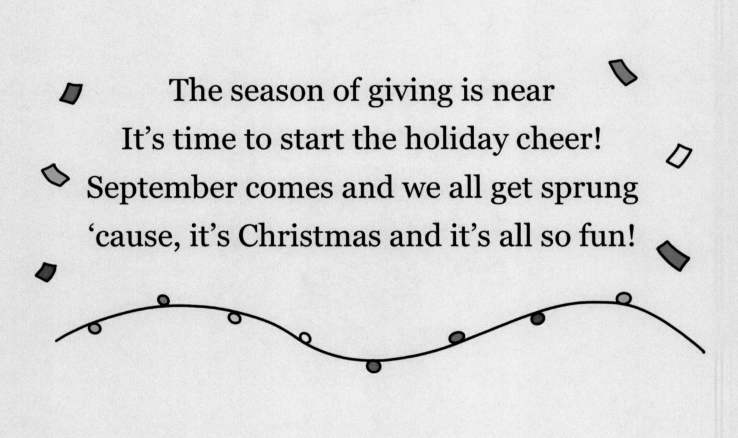

The season of giving is near
It's time to start the holiday cheer!
September comes and we all get sprung
'cause, it's Christmas and it's all so fun!

Lola's cooking up a feast,
mama's wrapping gifts,
We're all giddy during this
season
We get to stuff our tummies
with *Lechon!*
Delicious *Lumpia* and *Queso de
Bola*
"It's a must!", said Lola!

This is it, *Pancit*!
The sweet dishes
we eat
All the desserts and
kakanin
*Leche flan, crema
de fruta*
Puto bumbong, and
bibingka!

We see the Parol as our guiding light

To remind us to hope even in the darkest of night

A symbol of the Filipino spirit

That no matter how far, this is the love we celebrate

And the culture we get to inherit!

The food, the presents, the love for each other,

But the best part for me is when we get together!

These gifts we open at midnight

Under the holiday tree's dim lights.

"Great job, Inggo!", said the teacher
"I want to celebrate Christmas early too!", said many

Bright light, shiny star, my *Parol,* part of my culture!
One of the many Filipino traditions that
I'll share with my friends in the future!

Bright light, shiny star, that's how I know

Christmas is not that far!

We are always spreading goodness and joy

And for us that is very *Pinoy!*

- the end -